THE JUNGLE BOOK

Written by Rudyard Kipling

Retold by Narinder Dhami

Illustrated by Alexandra Ball

Collins

CHAPTER 1

"It's time to go hunting," said Father Wolf as the full moon rose above the hills. Inside the cave the four squealing cubs were playing close to their mother.

"Wait!" Mother Wolf said, pricking up her ears. "Do you hear that noise, Father?"

Not far away, down by the river, the wolves could hear the angry, sing-song whine of a tiger who was hungry.

"Shere Khan is back in our hunting grounds!"
Father Wolf growled. Shere Khan was a cruel
and cunning tiger who was hated by the other animals
because he didn't follow their jungle laws.

Suddenly, the tiger's whine changed to
a humming purr.

"He isn't searching for deer meat tonight,"
Mother Wolf replied. "He's hunting humans."

"The law of the jungle forbids us to kill humans,"
Father Wolf said angrily. "But Shere Khan doesn't care!"

3

A fierce roar split the darkness as the tiger charged towards his victim. The four cubs were frightened and cuddled close to their mother.

The tiger howled, long, loud and angry.

"Shere Khan has missed!" the wolves gasped.

Father Wolf ran out of the cave. Somewhere in the darkness he could hear Shere Khan muttering to himself.

"That stupid tiger has burnt his feet on a woodcutter's campfire!" he shouted. "And the humans have escaped."

But Mother Wolf's tail was twitching. "Something's coming towards our cave!" she whispered.

There was a rustling in the bushes nearby and the great wolf crouched on his back legs, ready to spring. But to his amazement, he saw a little baby who was just old enough to walk. The baby looked up into the wolf's face and laughed.

"A man cub!" Father Wolf cried. "Left behind by the humans!"

"Bring him to me," Mother Wolf called.

Gently, Father Wolf picked the baby up in his jaws. He carried him into the cave and laid him next to his family.

"How little he is!" said Mother Wolf.

Suddenly the cave grew dark. Shere Khan had pushed his great, striped head and shoulders into the entrance, blocking out the moonlight.

"The man cub is mine!" he snarled, his roar filling the cave with thunder. "Give him to me!"

Mother Wolf sprang to her feet. "Never!" she cried. "He'll live with our pack."

"We'll see," the angry tiger snapped. "The man cub belongs to me. And as soon as I get the chance, I'll kill him!"

That baby was me.

Mother Wolf called me Mowgli, and this is my story.

CHAPTER 2

That night Father and Mother Wolf took me to the wolves'
meeting place, the Council Rock. Their leader lay on top
of the tall stone looking down at everyone. His name
was Akela.

   "We laid you in the middle of the circle of wolves,"
Mother Wolf told me when I was older. "You sat there
with the other cubs, and you weren't scared at all."

   The wolves were amazed to see a human baby.
Akela said nothing, but suddenly there was
a loud roar from behind
the rocks.

"The man cub is mine!" Shere Khan bellowed. "Give him to me! Why do you want him?"

Some of the wolves nodded their heads. "Why *do* we want a human cub?" they snarled.

"Who speaks for this cub?" Akela asked. "Two members of this pack who aren't his parents must speak up for him."

Mother Wolf was worried no one would come forward, but then an old brown bear called Baloo stood up.

"Let the human cub stay," Baloo said kindly. "I'll teach him our jungle laws, just as I teach your other cubs."

Suddenly a long, inky-black shadow dropped down into the circle from one of the trees. It was Bagheera the panther.

"I know I have no right to be here," he purred politely. "But I wish to speak up for the human cub. The law of the jungle says that the life of a cub may be bought for a price. Am I right?"

"You're right," Akela replied.

"Then I offer the pack some meat, freshly killed tonight," Bagheera went on, "in return for the human cub's life."

"Yes, let him run with our pack!" the wolves agreed, easily persuaded by the thought of fresh meat. With that, they ran off to eat Bagheera's offering, while Shere Khan roared with rage.

Since that night, ten summers had passed, and I'd grown big and strong. Baloo was teaching me the laws of the jungle. Bagheera watched over me, and so did my wolf family.

"You must always be on the lookout for Shere Khan," Mother Wolf told me every day. "He hates humans, and he's sworn to kill you."

But I wasn't afraid of Shere Khan!

CHAPTER 3

"It's too hot for lessons today, Baloo!" I grumbled.

"Mowgli, we haven't finished yet," Baloo said crossly, but I'd had enough. I ran off, found one of the jungle pools and dived into the clear, warm water.

I loved to swim, run and climb. I loved sleeping in the sun and eating the wild honey that dripped from the trees. Father Wolf taught me and my wolf brothers about the other animals, and Bagheera showed me how to hunt for food.

But Baloo made me repeat the laws of the jungle
a hundred times a day, and I was bored!

I heard the brown bear lumbering after me, calling
my name, so I jumped out of the pool. Shaking back
my long wet hair, I climbed quickly up the nearest tree.
To my surprise, there were several strange grey animals
sitting in the highest branches.

"Hello, human cub!" they chattered.

"Who are you?" I asked, because I'd never seen
them before.

"We're the monkeys!" they cried. "You're our brother
because you stand on your feet as we do. You could be
our leader some day."

"Me, a leader?" I gasped, surprised. "Thank you!"

Then I heard Bagheera calling me, so I slid back down
the tree. He was waiting with a stern-looking Baloo.

"Tell me what you've learnt today," said Bagheera,
patting my arm with his big paw.

"I learnt the Master Words so I can speak to all animals, birds and snakes," I replied, jumping onto Bagheera's back. "We're of one blood, you and I. And I can whistle them like a bird or hiss them like a snake."

"Now you don't have to fear anyone in the jungle, Mowgli," Baloo said proudly.

"Except Shere Khan," Bagheera muttered.

"I don't fear Shere Khan," I scoffed. "Soon I'll be the leader of my very own tribe, high up in the treetops."

Baloo frowned. "Have you been talking to the monkeys?" he snapped. "We have nothing to do with them. They lie and cheat, and they're vain and boastful."

"Baloo's right," Bagheera said. His eyes were as hard as green pebbles. "The monkeys don't follow the jungle laws. They do as they please because they're afraid of no one except Kaa, the mighty python. Keep away from them, Mowgli."

I felt ashamed and said no more. Instead I lay down between Baloo and Bagheera as I always did, for our midday nap.

The next thing I remember was feeling lots of hard, strong little hands grabbing my arms and legs. Then I was dragged up high into the air.

CHAPTER 4

"Put me down!" I yelled, but the monkeys swung away
through the treetops at breakneck speed, taking me with
them. I could hear my friends shouting my name, but we
were moving too fast for them to catch us.

My head spun and I felt sick and dizzy. The monkeys
whooped and cheered as they hurtled from tree to tree.
I was terrified they'd drop me. We were already far from
home. How could I escape?

I glanced up at the sky and saw Rann the Kite Bird
hovering ahead. Quickly I whistled the Master Words
Baloo had taught me, "We're of one blood, you and I!"

Rann looked very surprised to hear a human calling
to him.

"Tell Baloo and Bagheera where I'm headed!"
I shouted before the monkeys rushed me away.

17

After what seemed like hours, we arrived at a ruined city. On top of the hill was a great, roofless palace with marble courtyards, fountains and orange trees. I was sore, angry and very hungry, but the monkeys didn't offer me any food. They just ran about chattering and fighting with each other.

"Baloo and Bagheera were right," I muttered.
"These monkeys don't follow our jungle laws at all!"

I wondered if Rann the Kite Bird had delivered my message, and if my friends would come to rescue me.

Suddenly a black shape streaked across the courtyard. It was Bagheera! He raced straight into the crowd of monkeys and began to fight his way towards me.

"Bagheera!" I shouted with relief.

I guessed Baloo was coming too, but that he was too old and slow to keep up with the speedy panther. I rushed to help Bagheera, but four monkeys grabbed me and threw me inside an old marble summerhouse. I was trapped. Then I heard Baloo's voice outside.

"I'm here, Baloo!"

The sounds of the battle got louder, but then there was another noise I recognised. It was the long, soft hiss of a snake. Relieved, I guessed that my friends had brought Kaa, the mighty python, to help rescue me!

Just then, there was a loud crash as the summerhouse collapsed around me. Kaa had crushed the marble walls with his huge green and yellow coils.

I scrambled from the rubble and saw Bagheera, Baloo and Kaa all bleeding and wounded. The monkeys stood frozen with fear, their eyes fixed on the enormous snake.

"Thank you, my brothers," I said gratefully. "I was wrong. I should've listened to you." I hugged Baloo and Bagheera, and then turned to Kaa.

"We're of one blood, you and I," I hissed like a snake.

"Thank you, Little Brother," said Kaa, his eyes twinkling. "Now go home and I'll teach these monkeys a lesson!"

CHAPTER 5

"Mowgli, I've something to tell you," Bagheera said,
the day after my monkey adventure. He sounded very
worried. "Shere Khan's back!"

"I'm not afraid of him," I replied. "Akela and the pack
will protect me."

Bagheera put his paw on my shoulder. "Akela is old now,
Mowgli," he said quietly. "If he can no longer hunt for his
own food, he can't lead the pack. That's one of the jungle
laws. With Akela gone, Shere Khan will hunt you down."

"But the pack are my friends," I argued.

"Mowgli, some of the young wolves hate you just for being human." The panther stared sadly at me. "You know I was born in the royal zoo, but I escaped and returned to the jungle? One day you, too, must return to your own people."

"But why?" I asked, puzzled.

"Because you aren't safe here," Bagheera replied. "You must protect yourself. Go to the human village and steal some of the Red Flower that grows outside their huts. Shere Khan's afraid of it."

I knew the Red Flower was fire, and that all animals feared it. So I ran off immediately to the human village. As I crossed the plain, I could hear the sound of my pack out hunting.

"Akela didn't kill anything!" I heard the young wolves howl gleefully. "We're going to have a new leader at last!"

Now I knew that what Bagheera said was true. If he couldn't hunt for food, Akela couldn't be leader of the pack. Without his protection, Shere Khan would be free to kill me.

I crept towards the village. I didn't go there often because, although the humans looked like me, we weren't the same. Hidden behind a tree, I saw a boy scoop red-hot charcoal from a burning fire into a small pot. Warming his hands on the pot, he went to feed the cattle.

I jumped out, grabbed the pot from him and ran, with the boy's cries ringing in my ears. I didn't stop until I reached the Council Rock.

Akela was lying beside the tall stone, not on top of it, as he was no longer the pack's leader. My blood boiled when I saw Shere Khan strutting around with some of the young wolves. Quietly I sat down with Bagheera, Baloo and my wolf family, the fire pot between my knees.

"I've waited ten years for this moment," Shere Khan purred silkily. "Now I ask you again to let me have the man cub."

"He's our brother," Akela began.

"Don't listen to this toothless old fool!" Shere Khan roared. "We'll kill him as well as the man cub!"

"Yes, we hate him because he is a man – a man – A MAN!" some of the young wolves snarled. My heart sank as they gathered around Shere Khan. The tiger's tail was twitching with excitement.

"Mowgli, there's nothing we can do now except fight!" Bagheera whispered.

CHAPTER 6

I leapt to my feet. I was bursting with rage and sorrow because I'd never realised before how much some of the wolves hated me.

"You're not my brothers any longer!" I cried. "Yes, I'm a man cub, and I've brought the Red Flower with me to prove it. Here it is!"

I flung the fire pot on the ground and some of the red-hot charcoals rolled out. They lit a patch of dried grass, where flames sprang up. Shere Khan and the wolves shrank back in fear.

I grabbed a dead branch and thrust it into the flames. Instantly it caught alight. I whirled the branch above my head and sparks flew.

"Save Akela from death," Bagheera whispered. "He was always your friend."

I nodded. Grasping the burning branch, I strode towards Shere Khan. The tiger was so afraid of the flames, he couldn't move. His eyes were wide and terrified. I stopped and waved the branch right in front of him, singeing his whiskers.

"Get out of here, Shere Khan!" I shouted. "And take these wolves who hate me with you! No one's to harm Akela either, do you understand?" I ran around the circle of wolves, shaking the burning branch at them.

Howling with fear, Shere Khan and most of the pack ran off into the darkness. They were gone ... for now. But I knew Shere Khan would never give up hunting me.

At last there was only Akela, Bagheera, Baloo, my wolf
family and the older wolves left. Then something began
to hurt inside me, something I'd never felt before.
The pain was much, much worse than falling from
a tree and banging my head, or being bitten by ants.
I caught my breath as my eyes filled with tears.

"What's the matter with me?" I sobbed.
"Am I dying, Bagheera?"

"No, Mowgli," Bagheera replied gently.
"You're crying because you're sad to leave
the jungle. But it's the only way to keep
you safe."

I turned to my wolf family.

"You won't forget me, will you?" I gulped.

"Never!" said my wolf cub brothers.
"We'll visit you every night."

"Come and see us soon, Mowgli," said Father
and Mother Wolf sadly.
   "I will," I replied. "And when I do, I'll deal with
Shere Khan once and for all!"
   So, as the dawn was beginning to break,
I set off through the jungle alone, to the human village.

CHAPTER 7

When I reached the village, people came running out of the huts. They stared at me in amazement, looked me up and down and talked loudly to each other, but I couldn't understand what they were saying.

"They're worse than the chattering monkeys!" I thought.

I opened my mouth and pointed at it to show I was hungry, but no one took any notice. Then a woman pushed her way through the crowd. She took my hand and led me away to her house.

I'd never been inside a house before, and I didn't know the names of any of the things there, or what they were for. The woman, who was called Messua, was very kind. She gave me bread and milk and named me Nathoo. I tried to tell her my name was Mowgli, but she couldn't understand me. I found out later that many years ago, her baby son Nathoo had been captured by Shere Khan. Messua thought I might be him, and that I'd come home at last.

That first night I felt trapped because I'd never slept under a roof before. I'd always gone to bed outdoors, under the dark, starry sky. So I jumped out of the window and went to sleep in the field.

I stretched out in the long, sweet-smelling grass and closed my eyes. But then a soft nose poked me under my chin.

"Grey Brother!" I cried, leaping up to hug him. He was the oldest of Father and Mother Wolf's cubs. "It's so good to see you."

"I bring news," Grey Brother said, sitting beside me. "Shere Khan's gone to hunt far away until his whiskers grow back. Then he's sworn to return and kill you."

"I'll be ready for him," I replied. "I'm very tired tonight, Grey Brother. There's so much to learn here. But I want to know all the jungle news. Do you see that rock?" I pointed to a tall rock on the other side of the plain.

"I'll look there for you or one of my brothers every day. If I don't see you, I'll know this is a sign Shere Khan's back."

Grey Brother nodded. "You won't forget you're a wolf?" he asked.

"Never!" I said. "I'll always love my wolf family. But the pack have cast me out because I'm a man cub."

"Remember, Mowgli, you may be cast out of the human pack, too," my brother replied quietly.

CHAPTER 8

"Mowgli the Jungle Boy!" The village children chased me down the street, calling me names. "Wolf Man!"

"Go away!" I shouted at them. "Just leaf me alone!"

They all burst out laughing. "You mean 'leave', not leaf!" one of the boys sneered. "You can't even speak properly!"

38

Three months had passed since I'd come to
the village, and every day I wished I was back in
the jungle. I was still learning the humans' language,
and I kept getting words wrong, although Messua tried
to teach me. I didn't understand the children's games,
so I couldn't join in with them. Anyway, they just called
me names and ran away from me.

I didn't understand their human laws, either.
Why did the village people wear so many clothes,
and what was the point of money? Why did the poor
people work so hard, while the rich people did nothing?
Messua was very kind to me, but I longed to go back
to my real home in the jungle.

Every night the head of the village and all the men would meet under the great fig tree to tell jungle tales. I soon realised they didn't know what they were talking about! Once I heard one of them telling a story about the ghost-tiger who'd stolen Messua's baby son.

I couldn't help laughing. "Shere Khan's no ghost-tiger," I said. "All your jungle stories are lies!"

The head man was very annoyed. "Tomorrow you'll do something useful and start herding the village cattle!" he snapped.

So every day, riding on the back of Rama the great bull, I took the cattle and the buffaloes out to the plains to graze. I lay under the trees while the cattle ate the grass and the buffaloes wallowed in the pools. I never forgot to check the tall rock. Every day one of my wolf brothers was there.

But then, one day, there was no one on top of the rock. Now I knew Shere Khan had returned, and that this time either he or I had to die.

CHAPTER 9

Immediately I leapt onto Rama's back and drove
the cattle and the buffaloes across the plain. When we
arrived at the tall rock, Grey Brother sprang out
of a clump of bamboo.

"Shere Khan's back?" I asked, my heart pounding
inside me. But I already knew the answer.

Grey Brother nodded. "He's hiding close by, in a deep,
narrow valley on the other side of the plain," he replied.
"He'll come for you at nightfall. But I've brought
a wise helper."

I turned and saw Akela padding towards us.

"Akela, I knew you wouldn't forget me!" I said
gratefully. "Listen, this is my plan. We'll divide the herd
in two and drive the cows and their calves one way,
the buffaloes the other. We'll block both ends of
the valley so Shere Khan can't escape."

"Good idea, Mowgli," Akela replied. "Once the cattle
get his scent, they'll charge to protect their calves."

Quickly we drove the herd across the plain to the valley. Grey Brother rounded up the cows and calves and led them to the high ground overlooking one end of the valley. Meanwhile, Akela and I herded the buffaloes to the other end. When all the animals were in place, I called, "Shere Khan!"

"Who's there?" the tiger snarled sleepily from behind the rocks.

"It's me, Mowgli!" I yelled.

At the sound of my voice, Shere Khan rushed out
from his sleeping place. Then I gave the signal to
Akela and Grey Brother. Both wolves began driving
their herds down the steep slopes into the valley.
Their heels drummed on the hard ground, sending up
clouds of dust. The noise echoed around the valley like
a thunderstorm.

Rama raced at the head of the buffaloes,
bellowing loudly. I clung tightly to
his neck, knowing he could smell
the scent of tiger.

For a moment, Shere Khan froze. The cattle were charging towards him from one end of the valley, the buffaloes from the other. Terrified, he ran for the valley walls to try to climb out, but they were too steep. I knew he was trapped.

Grunting and snorting, the two halves of the herd crashed headlong into each other in the middle of the valley, and Shere Khan disappeared under their stamping hooves.

47

CHAPTER 10

After the stampede, Akela and Grey Brother helped me to round up the buffaloes and the cattle, and then we led them back to the village. But when we arrived, there was a large crowd of angry people waiting for us.

"Sorcerer! Demon! Wolf cub!" they yelled at me. "Why do those wolves follow you, and do as you say? It must be evil magic!"

"Last time I was cast out it was because I'm a man," I sighed. "This time it's because I'm a wolf."

Quickly I said goodbye to Messua, who was crying, and then hurried away with Akela and Grey Brother. Night was falling and as I looked up at the milky moon, I felt happy.

"I'm back where I belong," I thought.

We went to the Council Rock and I spread Shere Khan's tiger skin on top of it. Bagheera, Baloo, Father and Mother Wolf and my brothers were glad to see me, and to hear that the tiger was dead.

"I knew that very first day when Shere Khan tried to push his way into our cave, that my Mowgli would hunt him down," Mother Wolf said, glowing with pride.

Akela called out for the other wolves to join us. Without his wise leadership, the pack had scattered far and wide. Some were lame from escaping hunters' traps; others were sick from eating rotten food.

"Lead us again, Akela," the wolves howled. "Lead us with Mowgli. We're ill and tired. We need wise and brave leaders."

But I shook my head. "The wolf pack and the human pack have both cast me out," I replied. "Now I'll hunt on my own."

"We'll come with you," said my wolf cub brothers.

So from that day on I went away and hunted in the jungle with my brothers. We had many adventures, but I often returned home to visit my best friends, Bagheera, Baloo and Akela. And I wasn't always alone because, later, I grew up and married and had human cubs of my own.

But that's another story!

THE LAWS OF THE JUNGLE

The Law Abiders

Bagheera

Akela

Mowgli

Baloo

Grey Brother

Mother and Father Wolf

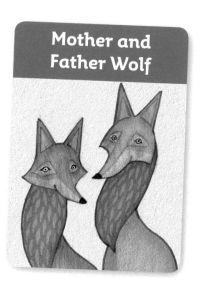

Kaa

The Lawbreakers

The wolves

The monkeys

Shere Khan

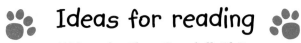

Ideas for reading

Written by Clare Dowdall, PhD
Lecturer and Primary Literacy Consultant

Reading objectives:
- make comparisons within and across books
- predict what might happen from details stated and implied
- summarise the main ideas drawn from more than one paragraph, identifying key details that support the main ideas

Spoken language objectives:
- participate in discussions, presentations, performances, role play, improvisations and debates

Curriculum links: Geography – locational knowledge; PSHE – relationships

Resources: ICT; pens and paper; materials for shadow puppets (dowling, split pins, tape and craft paper)

Build a context for reading

- Build vocabulary and a context for reading by asking children to describe what it's like in a jungle, and to make a list of creatures who live there.
- Look at the front cover. Ask children to share any prior knowledge about these famous stories by Rudyard Kipling, and to name the character in the illustration.
- Read the blurb with the children. Ask children to summarise the information in their own words. Discuss the phrase "the King of the jungle", and check that children understand what it means.

Understand and apply reading strategies

- Ask children to read Chapter 1 silently, or in pairs.
- Build a recount of the key events, using a comic strip or story map. Model how to note only significant moments in the recount.
- Using this aid, ask children to help you summarise the main points from Chapter 1 in their own words.